THE
REBELLIOUS
ALPHABET

Henry Holt and Company, Inc. / *Publishers since 1866* / 115 West 18th Street, New York, New York 10011

Translation copyright © 1993 by Geoffrey Fox / Text copyright © 1977 by Jorge Diaz /
Illustrations copyright © 1992 by Øivind S. Jorfald

Published in Canada by Fitzhenry & Whiteside Ltd., 195 Allstate Parkway, Markham, Ontario L3R 4T8. / Originally published in Norway by Carlsen Forlag, Oslo.

Library of Congress Cataloging-in-Publication Data
Diaz, Jorge. / [Alfabeto rebelde. English] / The rebellious alphabet / Jorge Diaz; illustrated by Øivind S. Jorfald; translated by Geoffrey Fox.
p.   cm.—(Edge graphics)
Summary: When an illiterate dictator bans all reading and writing, an old man
devises an ingenious system of printing messages and poems for the people.
[1. Literacy—Fiction. 2. Censorship—Fiction.] I. Jorfald, Øivind, ill. II. Title. III. Series.
PZ7.D544Re 1993 [Fic]—dc20   93-12697

ISBN 0-8050-2765-3
First American Edition—1993
Printed in the United States of America on acid-free paper. ∞
1 3 5 7 9 10 8 6 4 2

THE
REBELLIOUS
ALPHABET

· JORGE DIAZ ·

Translated by GEOFFREY FOX

Illustrated by ØIVIND S. JORFALD

HENRY HOLT AND COMPANY · NEW YORK

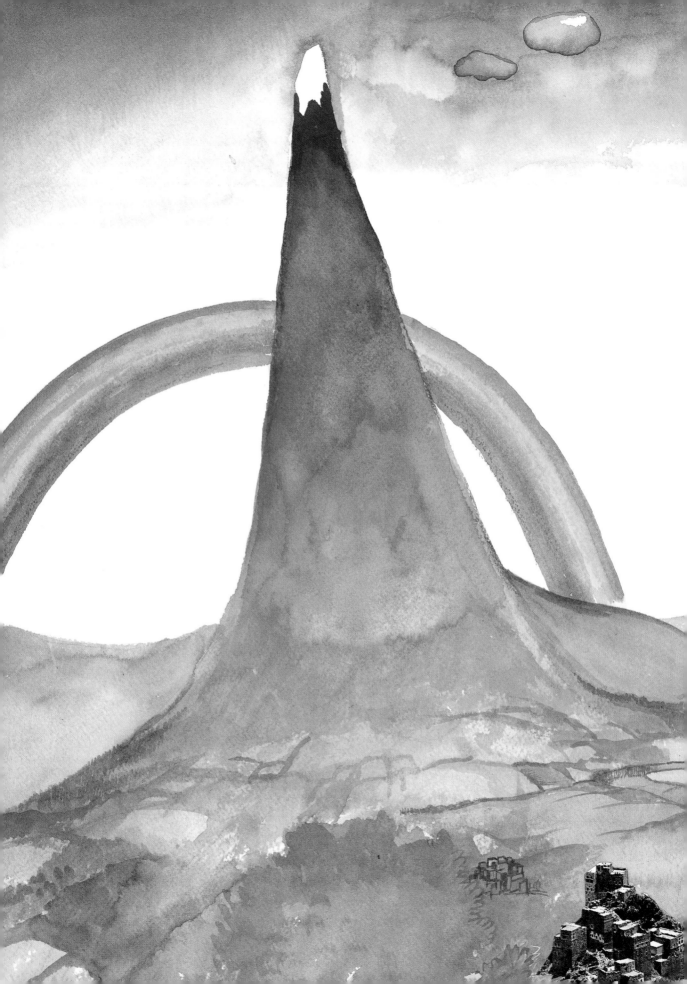

The Little General was the ruler of a very big village, even though he was very small.

He ruled the land by throwing temper tantrums and stomping his heels on the floor.

"Rodisflankis!! Conical gransifolopods!!

"Gratz and double-gratz!! Sclonch!!"

He shouted and everybody trembled, although they didn't understand a word he said.

The Little General was very ignorant. He didn't even know how to read and write. And because he wanted to be the master not just of the village but also of the minds and thoughts of the people who lived there, he banned reading. He banned writing and printing, too.

The only way the people in the village found out about what was happening in other parts of the world was from the Village Crier, who said only what the Little General ordered him to say.

"Hear ye! Hear ye! The world outside our village is a mess. There are earthquakes, floods, and criminals on the loose. But in our village there is peace, much peace, gallons of peace, pounds of peace, tons of peace. And now that you know that you are all happy, go and pay your taxes to the Little General!" cried the Crier.

But there was a little old man in the village who liked to read, who liked to write, and who wanted to be the master of his own thoughts. His name was Plácido, which means peaceful.

He lived in a basement full of plants and birds, because people who are free love nature.

Since the Little General had banned reading and writing, the old man had to invent a very ingenious system to print his poems, his letters, and his leaflets. This is how he did it:

He kept seven canaries inside a large cage. Every one of them had two letters of the alphabet and one punctuation mark on each foot.

So each canary carried four letters on its stiff toes.

When Plácido wanted to print anything, he would open the cage and his canaries would perch on a sponge full of ink that he held in his hand. Then the canaries would jump up and down on a sheet of white paper, forming the words of the poem or letter or protest leaflet.

The first paper he printed was just such a leaflet—a sort of hymn to liberty—and a gust of wind carried it out through the little window of the basement where Plácido worked. It rose in the air like a comet and landed in the middle of the village square.

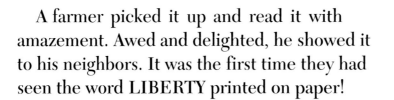

A farmer picked it up and read it with amazement. Awed and delighted, he showed it to his neighbors. It was the first time they had seen the word LIBERTY printed on paper!

Throughout the day the wind carried many other papers over the village. All the people living in the village talked about what was on the papers that had been printed by the little feet of Plácido's canaries. They understood, for the first time, that the Little General was tiny and ignorant.

The Little General lived in a castle, in the highest part of the village, and from there he constantly watched over each and every one of the villagers through a telescope that was three times as long as he was. Because he watched them all the time, he could see the commotion the pieces of paper were causing and the rejoicing of the people.

He ordered his men to bring some of the papers.

"Pringa rongo pluckus doublequick!! Slammettybang!! Growf!!"

His armed men ran into the village and brought him a few of the troublesome pages. When he had them in his hands, the Little General scratched his head again and again. He didn't understand a single word. He didn't know how to read, but he didn't want anybody to know that. He turned the papers around, right side up and backward, sideways and other-sideways, but he couldn't make out even a single letter.

Furious and ashamed of his own ignorance, the Little General ordered his soldiers to find the secret printing press, even if they had to look under every stone.

"Glup . . . scrunch shpf last!"

And they all trembled because they understood it was a terrifying command.

The soldiers asked the villagers, but nobody told them anything. They opened doors and climbed up to the weather vanes and the belfries, frightening the storks . . . but they didn't find the press.

When the soldiers were on their way back to the castle, they saw a printed sheet of white paper whirling up in the air from a basement window. And that was how they discovered our friend Plácido, surrounded by papers, writing verses about liberty.

Before he was taken off to jail, Plácido asked the soldiers to let him take his canaries with him because their songs made him happy. The soldiers, who were really good farm boys like Plácido himself, winked and agreed. Plácido was locked up in a dungeon of the castle, and from there he could hear the dreadful orders of the Little General.

"Kleenshweep brinkshpot!! Broomboom shplonket!!"

This meant that his soldiers were supposed to sweep up all the letters they found in the village. The alphabet was to be done away with!

Without any enthusiasm, just the way they might carry their machine guns, the soldiers picked up their brooms and went through the village, sweeping up letters.

They carried out their task so well that, while sweeping up the letters on the printed papers and leaflets, they also swept up the letters on the signs in the village, such as "Butcher Shop," "Bakery," "Village Square," "Olive Tree Lane," and even a little sign that said "No Garbage Dumping."

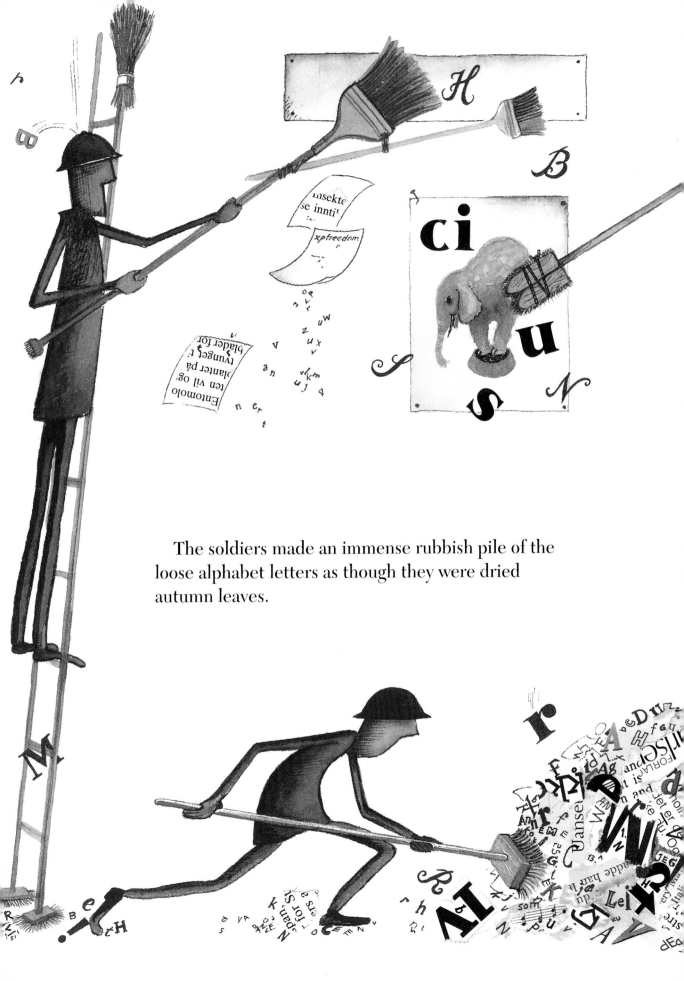

The soldiers made an immense rubbish pile of the loose alphabet letters as though they were dried autumn leaves.

When there were no more letters to sweep up
in the whole village, the Little General in person
set fire to the rubbish heap of
letters. Poems, protests,
and history disappeared
in the flames.

More than one villager shed a
silent tear while watching
the bonfire, but the tears
did not put out the fire
of ignorance.

The black smoke from the ink of the burned letters rose to the sky and formed a cloud that hovered precisely over the castle. The Little General thought it was nighttime and went off to bed.

"Gulp bang trinca kaput!" he said, and started to snore.

Then, unexpectedly, through the smoke and their sorrowful silence, the people began to hear the sound of Plácido's canaries.

If the canaries were singing, it meant that they had gotten out of their cage,

and if they were out of the cage, it meant that they were jumping from side to side with their alphabet feet.

And in fact, even inside his cell, the little old man was printing his papers with the help of his singing, literate canaries. Their ink-spattered feet were drawing the beautiful pattern of ideas.

"Umug . . . Lopside idinumskulls!! Orolipidous remantragores!!"

The Little General had woken up and ordered his soldiers to set Plácido free because the continuous singing of the typesetting canaries kept him awake. He never did find out that the noise disturbing his sleep was really a printing shop, and that the printers worked day and night to bring words of hope to the village.

Thunder rumbled and lightning flashed, and the black cloud that had formed from the burned letters was split apart and unleashed a storm.

Black ink poured down over the castle. The Little General ran up to the tower to see what was happening. As he looked through his enormous spyglass, the ink fell on his clothes and made parallel stripes so that it looked as though he were wearing a prisoner's uniform. Seeing that, the soldiers laughed and left the castle.

It also rained on the village.

The ink fell on the walls of the houses and formed letters and words: "Liberty" . . . "Village" . . . The letters came together again on blank pieces of paper. As though they were happy little bugs, they climbed the walls and began to form names and labels: "Fresh Eggs" . . . "Shoe Repair" . . . "Dairy Products" . . .

Then the storm ended and the sun came out.

The people came out of their houses. They read Plácido's verses and understood that the Little General would never leave the castle again because he had a striped suit and was embarrassed.

And now Plácido's basement has been turned into a library, and the villagers use the Little General's telescope to look at the stars.